EGMONT

We bring stories to life

First published in Great Britain in 2007 by Dean,
an imprint of Egmont UK Limited
239 Kensington High Street, London W8 6SA

Thomas the Tank Engine & Friends™

A BRITT ALLCROFT COMPANY PRODUCTION

Based on The Railway Series by The Reverend W Awdry
Photographs © 2007 Gullane (Thomas) LLC. A HIT Entertainment Company

Thomas the Tank Engine & Friends and Thomas & Friends are trademarks of Gullane (Thomas) Limited.
Thomas the Tank Engine & Friends and Design is Reg. US. Pat. & Tm. Off.

ISBN 978 0 6035 6257 0
ISBN 0 6035 6257 4
1 3 5 7 9 10 8 6 4 2
Printed in Singapore

Bulgy Rides Again

The Thomas TV Series

DEAN

Summertime is always a busy time for the engines on the Island of Sodor. They carry visitors around all day long.

But one summer the engines had a problem.

Thomas and Emily were in the foundry for repairs so the other engines had to work *extra* hard.

"Oh, my aching axles!" grumbled Gordon, as he passed Percy.

"I must find a way for us to carry more passengers," said The Fat Controller to Thomas and Emily. "We have more visitors than ever this year!"

"And fewer engines," chuffed Emily.

"It's a double-decker problem," smiled Thomas.

But The Fat Controller didn't laugh. "That's just given me an idea!" he said.

Bulgy was a big double-decker bus. He had been made into a hen house after his naughty behaviour caused a crash. The Fat Controller drove straight to Bulgy's field.

"Hello, Bulgy," said The Fat Controller. "How would you like to be back on the road again?"

Bulgy was very excited.

"Thank you, Sir!" he cried. "I'll be the best bus ever!"

Thomas was surprised to see Bulgy.

"I'm going back on the road," explained Bulgy.

"Good for you!" said Thomas. "The farmer needs a van to deliver his vegetables around the Island."

"Vegetables?" said Bulgy, crossly.

"I'm not carrying silly old *vegetables*. I'm carrying *passengers*!"

Soon Bulgy looked as good as new. He had been refitted and had a shiny new coat of paint.

When he went back to his field, he tooted proudly at the hens.

"We'll start in the morning," said his Driver. "Goodnight, Bulgy!"

Bulgy smiled happily.

That night, Bulgy dreamed about how smart he would look in the morning, full of passengers.

But the hens missed their old home! One by one, they crept into his luggage racks and soon were fast asleep.

In the morning, Bulgy set off bright and early to pick up his first passengers. There were lots of people waiting!

"All aboard!" tooted Bulgy, and he set off for Knapford Station. He drove so smoothly that the sleepy hens didn't wake up!

Trevor was on the road ahead, chugging along slowly.

"Get a move on, slowcoach!" called Bulgy, importantly. "I've got passengers on board!"

Bulgy started to overtake Trevor, but suddenly, he saw the mail truck coming the other way!

"Oh, no!" cried Bulgy.

Bulgy swerved and missed the mail truck. But the swerving woke the hens up – and they were very frightened! They flapped and they squawked loudly!

"Stop!" complained the passengers. "We want to get off!"

The passengers were furious. They were covered in feathers and broken eggs.

Bulgy was covered in eggs and feathers, too. He had to go to the washdown to be cleaned.

"Horrid hens! Pesky passengers!" grumbled Bulgy. "It's not my fault!"

"We've been repaired now," said Thomas. "We'll be back carrying passengers again."

"But the farmer still needs a van to carry his vegetables," sighed Emily.

That gave Bulgy an idea.

"I don't like hens *or* passengers," Bulgy told The Fat Controller. "Could I help the farmer instead?"

The Fat Controller chuckled. Now Thomas and Emily were back, he had enough engines to carry passengers.

"All right, Bulgy," he said. "You'll be the Island's only vegetable stand on wheels!

And that's just what happened! Bulgy was repainted and lots of people came to buy vegetables from him.

Sometimes, Bulgy sees Thomas with carriages full of passengers but he's not jealous. He likes working with vegetables – they don't lay eggs, and they never complain!